BRAVE KIDS
True Stories from America's Past

Robert Henry Hendershot

BRAVE KIDS
True Stories from America's Past

Robert Henry Hendershot

Susan E. Goodman
Illustrated by Doris Ettlinger

Aladdin
New York   London   Toronto   Sydney   Singapore

First Aladdin edition March 2003

ALADDIN PAPERBACKS
An imprint of Simon & Schuster Children's Publishing Division
1230 Avenue of the Americas
New York, NY 10020

Also available in an Aladdin Paperbacks edition

Designed by Lisa Vega
The text of this book was set in Palatino.

Printed in the United States of America
10 9 8 7 6 5 4 3 2 1

Library of Congress Control Number 2002107334

ISBN 0-689-84981-8

To Marjorie Waters—a great reader,
an even better friend

Acknowledgments

I'd like to thank Walter Estabrook, Tom Nanzig, and Dave Finney for knowing so much about the Civil War. Thanks to Walter for his knowledge of the details, Tom for his invaluable research, and Dave for all his help with Robert and the use of his photo.

Thanks to readers Liza Ketchum, Lisa Jahn-Clough, and Janet Coleman for all their insights. Doris Ettlinger for bringing another story into view. And, to Molly McGuire and Ellen Krieger for their constant support.

Table of Contents

Chapter One

War Fever!

The minute that war was declared, Robert knew he had to fight.

America's southern states wanted to become their own country called the Confederate States of America. The northern states wanted them to stay in the Union.

Robert was itching to fight the southern rebels. He had what Ma called "war fever."

Ma said Robert had to stay in school. Robert was only twelve. He was too young to join the army.

Robert watched the older boys in town sign up. They were forming a group of soldiers called a company.

They don't have to go to school, thought Robert. *Why should I?*

He followed the new soldiers to the edge of town. He watched them drill.

Forward march. Left foot, right foot, left then right.

One day Robert brought a piece of wood.

It was long and thin, just like a musket.

Left foot, right foot, left then right. Robert marched alongside the soldiers.

Finally Captain DeLand gave in.

"Robert Henry Hendershot," he called. "Fall in line."

From then on Robert practiced with the soldiers all the time. He marched up and down. He faced right and left. He learned to shoulder his wooden musket.

Soon it was time for the soldiers to leave.

When they left, Robert left too.

But not for long. A month later, he was on a train. Captain DeLand was taking him back home to Jackson, Michigan.

"Please let me stay with you, Captain DeLand," said Robert.

"No, Robert," the captain said. "A twelve-year-old boy cannot be a soldier."

"I march as well as anyone," Robert protested.

"You do, lad," the captain agreed. "But I said I'd bring you back to your mother."

The train began to slow down. Its whistle blew.

"Jackson station!" the conductor called. "Jackson is next!"

"Captain DeLand, I'll do anything!" Robert cried.

Captain DeLand liked Robert's spirit. If all his soldiers had it, the war would soon be won.

"Go home and talk to your mother," he said at last. "If she agrees, I will let you join us. You can be our drummer boy."

Robert didn't need to go home to find his mother. She was waiting on the platform. She wrapped her arms around him.

"Robert, I've been so worried!" she cried. Her voice was happy and angry at the same time.

"Ma," he said. He hugged her back.

Robert didn't want to be in Jackson. But he was very glad to see his mother.

He didn't ask about the army at the station. He didn't want the captain to hear her answer.

"Let's go home," he said.

Chapter Two

Home Again

We could have stayed at the station, Robert thought later. *She is yelling so loud, the whole town can hear!*

But Robert didn't give up.

"Ma, please," he begged. "I have to go."

"War is not a game, Robert," she said. "It is dangerous."

"Papa would understand why I need to go," he shouted.

Both of them were quiet for a moment. They were thinking of Robert's father, who had died years before.

"Papa would want you to grow up to be a man," Ma said finally. "He would not want you to die—a boy on a battlefield."

Ma pushed her lips together. They drew a straight line across her face.

"I will never let you go," she said.

Robert hung his head. His shoulders sank. He turned and walked away.

The next morning, Robert walked into the kitchen.

"Ma, do you need some wood for the stove?" he asked.

Robert's mother turned around. She looked at her son very carefully.

Why is he so cheerful? she wondered.

"We could use some wood," was all she said.

Robert stacked some logs by the stove. He was whistling the song, "Yankee Doodle."

"There's apple pie for breakfast," Ma said.

"Great," said Robert. "I missed your pie!"

Ma looked at Robert carefully again. But she smiled as he cut a second piece.

Robert spent the morning doing chores. He fed the chickens. He brought in the eggs.

He was carrying water in from the well when he heard the whistle. Another train was coming through town.

Robert took the pail to the sink. He poured water into Ma's dishpan.

The whistle tooted again.

"I haven't seen my friend Frank for a long time," said Robert. "I think I'll go visit him."

Ma didn't even look up. She was busy peeling potatoes.

"Be home in time for dinner," she said.

Later, Ma finished kneading the bread. She put it in the window to rise. That's when she saw the train pulling out of the station. It was filled with soldiers.

"Oh, no!" she cried. She dashed out, leaving her cake to burn in the oven.

Ma ran to the tracks. She burst into tears.

Robert was leaning out of a train window. He was waving to everyone he saw.

The train slowly picked up speed. Then Robert saw his mother.

"Don't cry, Ma," he called. "I'll write when I get to camp."

Ma finally understood that she could not stop him.

"Good-bye, Robert," she said. "Pray often."

The whistle blew.

And Robert's train chugged off.

Chapter Three

The Fight Begins

I wonder if Ma is still mad at me, Robert thought.

He poked at the campfire.

"Soon she'll be proud," he said out loud.

"Papa too," he whispered.

Robert stirred the kettle hanging over the fire. Yesterday he had used it to wash the bugs out of clothing. Now it held stew. At first Robert hated this idea. He didn't even think about it anymore.

Robert had become a real soldier. He

hadn't had a piece of pie in months. Now he ate hardtack, crackers so hard that soldiers called them "teethdullers." He pounded coffee beans with a rifle butt and boiled them for breakfast.

When he marched he never missed a beat. He helped others keep in step with his drum. Pounding different rhythms on his drum helped the soldiers know what to do. Troop Call ordered, "Get into line." The Call to Arms told the guards to hurry to their posts.

Robert and his company had joined a bigger group called a regiment. Many, many regiments had come together to form a big army. Thousands and thousands of Union soldiers were camped on the Rappahannock River in Virginia.

The Confederate Army waited on the other side, near the town of Fredericksburg.

Today, Robert thought, *my drum will call our regiment into battle.*

He took a moment to imagine what would happen. Cannons would roar. Gun smoke would blacken the air. When the soldiers could not hear an order, Robert's drum would tell them to get their muskets ready. When they could not see, his drum would tell them to fire!

I am ready, Robert decided.

Robert was ready. His army was not. They had no way to cross the river.

All night the army had worked to build a bridge. Men placed big pontoon boats side by side. Then they tied them together. They had enough boats to stretch across the river to Fredericksburg. Wooden boards across the boats would turn them into a bridge.

In the darkness the men built the bridge

most of the way across. At dawn they had only eighty more feet to go. But at dawn the rebels could see to aim their rifles.

In the early morning light, a band of men picked up some boards. They ran out to finish the bridge.

Crack! Crack! Crack! went the Confederate rifles.

The men fell headfirst into the river.

Robert heard the cries of anger from the soldiers on shore. He could not see what was happening. He grabbed his drum. He left his own regiment behind and ran to the river.

"This is murder!" he heard a general say. "We are sending men out to be shot by the rebs hiding in houses."

More brave men tried to finish the bridge. *Crack! Crack! Crack!* More brave men died. General Burnside was the general in charge of the whole army. "This is hopeless," he said. "There is only one way to get those sharpshooters out of hiding."

"Shell the city!" General Burnside ordered. "Batter it down!"

Chapter Four

The Battle of the Bridges

The Union cannons began to thunder. One hundred and fifty angry guns fired through clouds of smoke.

The ground is shaking, Robert thought. *It feels like an earthquake.*

A storm of metal went howling across the river. Shells tore holes in brick houses. They battered down walls. Barns crumpled into sticks and twigs.

A wooden house burst into flames. Fire shot into the sky. Robert watched the smoke rise up in thick, black columns.

"Take that, you traitors," he yelled.

The cannons roared again and again. Soon Robert could not see what was happening in Fredericksburg. Black smoke hid everything but flames.

For two whole hours the cannons fired upon Fredericksburg. Then the thunder stopped.

Union soldiers stared at the clouds across the river. They waited for the smoke to clear.

"Fredericksburg might have been beautiful," one soldier finally said. "It is not beautiful now."

"And not a graycoat to be seen!" Robert added.

The Union cheers were almost as loud as their cannons. But the soldiers didn't waste time celebrating. They had a bridge to build.

"I'll go," cried one soldier. He picked up a board and set out across the pontoon bridge.

Crack! Crack! Crack! went the rebel rifles.

Another soldier fell.

"They are still in their hiding places," Robert shouted.

Sure enough, Confederate shooters were still in the ruined houses. They also hid behind a hill close to shore.

Then the Union soldiers understood that their cannons could never get the sharpshooters. Men had to drive the rebels from their hiding places. Only then could the bridge be finished.

"We must send soldiers across in boats," said one general.

The men knew this was a very dangerous mission. Boats crossing the river were very easy targets.

"Who will volunteer?" the general said.

"We'll do it," cried the soldiers from the Seventh Michigan regiment.

"So will we," shouted two groups from Massachusetts.

"And me," said Robert, although his regiment was not even there.

The men ran down to ten pontoon boats waiting on a wagon. A minute before, these pontoons were going to be part of the bridge. Now they were boats for the attack.

The great Union cannons boomed once more. Their shells kept the enemy busy. The soldiers had a chance to get ready.

The men of the Seventh Michigan regiment pulled the boats to the riverbank.

Robert was the first to climb in.

Chapter Five

"Ready to Go!"

At last, Robert thought, *here is my big chance!*

A dozen soldiers rushed onto each pontoon. Some of them picked up the heavy oars. Others grabbed long wooden poles.

Robert watched the soldiers come into his boat. One dropped the regiment's flag into a corner. Others put their muskets in a pile and kept moving. They all took their places.

Robert did not know any of them. Still, they felt like his best friends.

"Ready!" shouted the men from one boat.

"Ready!" "Ready!" "Ready!" cried soldiers from the other pontoons.

"Ready to go!" Robert yelled for his crew.

The captain turned at the sound of his young voice.

"Boy," he said, "what are you doing in there?"

"Going to fight the rebs, sir," Robert answered.

"Oh no, you're not," said the captain. "Come back on shore!"

Robert did not say a word. He did not move an inch.

"Son, you are too small for this business," the captain said. "You will be killed."

Robert got up. He stood as tall as his twelve-year-old body would let him.

"I am willing to die for my country," he said.

"But I am not willing to let you," said the captain. "Out! Now!"

Robert stared at his feet. It wasn't his fault he was so young. He felt ashamed anyway.

Then Robert had an idea. His face brightened. He climbed over oar and musket. Once he was on shore, he turned to the captain.

"Sir, can I help push off?" he asked.

The captain had already moved on toward his next problem.

"Can I help push the boat into the water?" Robert asked again.

"I suppose," the captain called over his shoulder.

Soon all the boats were loaded. It was time to go.

"Let's go, men," cried the captain.

Many Union soldiers rushed forward.

They ran to the pontoons and began to push. Robert's face turned red with the effort. The boats inched forward. Thousands of men on the hills behind them began to cheer.

Ten pontoons entered the Rappahannock. The soldiers pushing them waded back to shore. All but Robert.

Robert never let go of his pontoon. He found the edge covered by the regiment's flag. He reached under the flag and grabbed the boat.

As the pontoons started across the Rappahannock, Robert's body sank into the river. No one in the boat—or on shore—even noticed him.

"Bless you, lads!" shouted the captain.

Bless me, too, Robert thought.

The icy water swirled over Robert's shoulders. His drum floated by his side.

Chapter Six

Cold Crossing

At first the boats drifted slowly. Then the rowers began to work together. Men with poles dug into the river bottom. They pushed the boats forward too. Cheers from the shore helped them all work harder.

The oars dipped into the water. Again and again. Every stroke took them closer to danger.

"Faster, men!" shouted a soldier on Robert's boat. "We're late for our appointment with Johnny Reb!"

Robert felt his boat pick up speed.

Faster is right, he thought. *It's so cold in here.*

His teeth began to chatter.

"We're halfway there," said a soldier.

Robert could hear thumping in the boat above him. Men were reaching for their muskets.

The flag covering Robert's hands kept him from being seen. It didn't keep him warm, though. His hands were so cold that he could hardly hold on.

"Keep low, boys," he heard someone say. "No need to give them an easy target."

I'm freezing, he thought. *Still, I am being careful, Ma. The river is the safest place to be.*

Crack! Crack! Crack! Rebel guns began to fire.

Robert heard a thud and a moan. "Take

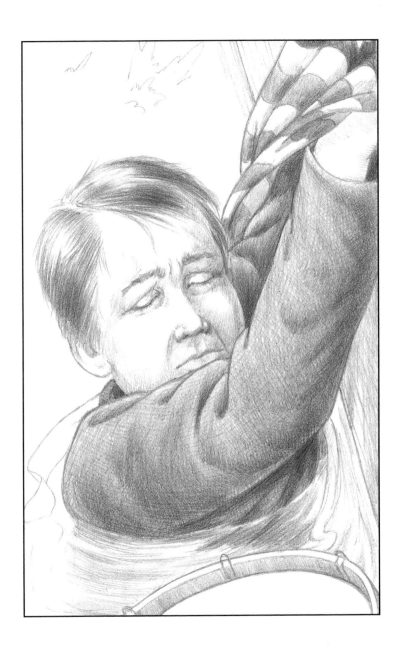

over the oar," a soldier yelled. The boat rocked as men changed places.

But it kept on moving.

Robert saw little splashes of water all around him.

It looks like rain, he thought. *Rain made of lead, not water.*

Another cry. Another moan. Then a scream.

The boat kept on moving.

Robert closed his eyes. He could still hear the shouts and the hissing bullets. He heard the groans and the prayers. Still, shutting his eyes made the sounds seem farther away.

I can't even feel my toes, Robert thought. *I wonder if I ever will again.*

Then his feet bumped something—the river bottom. Soldiers jumped out of the boat. They began to wade toward shore.

Some of them got hit by bullets. They lay half floating in the water.

Robert let go of the boat. He bent down low and moved toward shore. His drum floated behind him.

Robert stayed covered by water as long as possible. When he reached the riverbank, he stopped. He took a few deep breaths. He tried to stop shivering.

"Now!" he shouted. He scrambled onto the shore. He stood and began to run.

Robert felt something push him off his feet. He was knocked to the ground.

"Oh no," he cried. "I've been hit!"

Chapter Seven

On the Attack

Robert lay still for a moment. Then he moved his legs. His arms were next. He patted his chest. He felt his face. He seemed all right.

I feel fine, he thought. *So what happened?*

Robert got up and then he saw.

"My drum!" he moaned.

A bullet had blasted the drum into pieces.

Robert grabbed a chunk of the drum. He threw it as hard as he could.

I wish that was a bullet, he thought. *A cannon ball to blow up this whole town!*

Suddenly Robert wasn't cold anymore. His heart was pounding so hard that he could feel it. It felt like the beat of his drum.

Robert forgot about being scared. He was angry.

Robert wasn't sure what he was going to do. But he knew he had to get into Fredericksburg.

Robert hadn't gone far before he came upon a fallen soldier. A man from the Seventh Michigan had been shot and killed.

Robert was so ready to fight that he didn't even feel sad. He just picked up the soldier's musket.

It's still loaded, he thought. *I'll use it for both of us.*

Robert stayed low to the ground. He dragged the musket beside him. It measured over six feet from its butt to the tip of its bayonet. It was much taller than he was.

Robert rushed up the riverbank. Many men from the Seventh Michigan were already there. They had run to the homes facing the river.

Light flashed in the windows of the houses. This fire came from Confederate guns. Union soldiers were smashing in doors. They were trying to get at the rebels inside.

I'm going to find a house of my own, thought Robert.

Robert snuck down the street, struggling to carry the heavy musket. He eyed every yard on his way. He carefully walked by each woodpile. He knew they could be hiding places for Confederate sharpshooters.

Soon Robert came upon a big wooden house. Two days ago it was a house Robert would have loved to live in. But it too had

been in battle. Union cannons had knocked in its chimney. Its windows were shattered. A shell had taken a bite from its side.

This is a good one to explore, he thought.

Robert lifted his musket and went inside.

There, in the parlor, was a tall rebel soldier. He was looking out the window. He had fired his rifle so often that his face was all black from powder.

He looks more like a demon than a man, Robert thought.

The man was getting ready to fire again. He had squeezed a bullet into his gun barrel.

Robert did not waste a second.

He swung the musket all the way up, even though it was very heavy. He cocked the hammer. He pointed its bayonet right at the man's chest.

"Surrender!" he cried.

Chapter Eight

The Drummer Boy of the Rappahannock

The rebel soldier spun around. He saw a boy standing there. He saw the musket staring right at him. He saw that it was ready to be fired.

"Don't shoot," the graycoat cried.

He threw his rifle to the floor. He slowly raised his arms up high.

Robert remembered the captain's parting words.

"Use your bayonets, boys," the captain had commanded. "Show no mercy."

Robert looked at his prisoner. He was very thin. His gray coat had been patched many times.

Yes, he is a rebel, Robert thought. *He is also a man.*

"Keep your hands up," Robert said. "We're going outside."

The rebel moved toward the door. Robert fell in behind him. His bayonet pointed right between his prisoner's shoulders. The two of them marched back toward the river.

The rest of the Seventh Michigan had been busy as well. Using rifle butts, bullets, and bayonets, they had captured Sophia Street. They had forced the sharpshooters out of cellars. Out of barns. Out from kitchens and hallways.

As soon as Robert saw the group on Sophia Street, he began to grin.

They didn't obey orders either, he thought. *There are more prisoners than our boys in blue.*

When the Seventh Michigan saw Robert and his prize, they were amazed.

"Hip, hip, hurrah!" someone shouted. "Three cheers for the Drummer Boy of the Rappahannock!"

The soldiers clapped and waved their arms. They whooped and hollered.

Robert smiled. He whispered a "hurrah" of his own. But he never lowered his weapon. Not one inch, even though that ten-pound musket seemed to weigh a ton.

"Do you need some help guarding your prisoner?" asked another soldier.

Robert lifted his musket even higher.

"No," he answered proudly, "I am enough for him."

The men of the Seventh Michigan weren't

the only ones working hard. The bridge across the Rappahannock was almost done. All the pontoons were in place. The last boards were being tied across them.

Even before the bridge was ready, the Union soldiers started crossing. Robert watched lines and lines of them march by.

As they passed, many of them called out.

"Look at the drummer boy!"

"Hurrah for the drummer boy!"

"He is a real soldier now!"

At last it was Robert's turn to use the bridge. He and his prisoner crossed to the Union side of the river. They marched over to where soldiers were taking their prisoners. Only then did Robert lower his musket.

Just at that moment, General Burnside was walking by. He saw Robert give up his captive. He listened to Robert's story.

Despite the dangerous battle ahead, Burnside smiled. For a moment he could forget ordering 120,000 men to risk their lives.

"Boy, I glory in your spunk," Burnside said. "If you keep on in this way a few more years, you will be in my place."

Chapter Nine

March 15, 1864

"Calm down," Robert ordered himself.

You have seen men shot, he thought. *You have been shot at yourself.*

Robert took a deep breath. He slowly let it out in a sigh.

"This makes me even more nervous," he muttered.

Robert squirmed in his seat. His foot tapped the flowery carpet. His fingers played softly on his new drum.

Robert smiled. Just touching his drum made him feel better.

He rubbed its hoops of rosewood. They looked so beautiful against the shell of glowing silver.

Rap-tap-tap went his fingers. The drumheads were so clear Robert could see his new pants right through them.

For the thousandth time, Robert looked at the words engraved on the drum's side. "To Robert Henry Hendershot," he read, "for his gallantry at the Attack on Fredericksburg, eleventh December, 1862."

Rap-tap-tap. So much had happened since Robert marched his prisoner across that bridge.

Who would guess I'd be out of the army three weeks later, he thought. *Spared from a bullet, but shot down by illness.*

Rap-tap-tap. Then there were all those newspaper stories about him. And that poem. Mama was so proud after all.

Robert stared ahead. He was trying to remember the poem that was written about him. Instead he found himself looking at the curtains. Other visitors had cut strips out of them as souvenirs.

He looked at the ceiling instead.

"I've got it," he said.

" 'Soldiers on the shore, with the bayonet and gun, though the drum could beat no more, made the dastard rebels run,' " he recited to himself.

" 'Made the dastard rebels run!' " he repeated.

To finish the poem, Robert quietly tapped out the chammade. This drumbeat told soldiers it was time to fight.

The door near Robert opened. Robert jumped up.

I guess that was too loud, he thought. *I'm in trouble now!*

A man walked over to Robert. He was wearing a long coat of Union blue. It was spotless. Robert knew it had never seen battle. Its bright brass buttons had never been scratched by carrying a musket.

Robert stood straight and tall. He tried to press the wrinkles out of his jacket.

"Come with me," the man said. "President Lincoln will see you now."

The first thing Robert saw was a long wooden table covered with books and letters. Maps of the battlefronts hung on the wall. Oilcloth protected the floor from men who spit and wore dirty boots.

Robert searched the room. There he was. He was sitting in a black chair near the window.

When Abraham Lincoln stood, he seemed to go up forever.

"Ah, Captain Robert Henry Hendershot, the famous Drummer Boy of the Rappahannock," said President Lincoln, holding out his hand. "It is an honor!"

"Thank you, sir," said Robert.

"Sit down," said Lincoln. "Tell me all about it."

Robert told the president about being in the Rappahannock. He described the streets of Fredericksburg.

He also told Lincoln about his year after leaving the army. He had gone home for a while. He had tried school for a while too. He even became an attraction at P. T. Barnum's museum. People came from near and far to hear his story. And to see him play his drum.

"Well," said Lincoln, "it's quite a drum."

"Yes," said Robert proudly. "The *Tribune*

newspaper company gave it to me. They said it would replace the one I lost."

The circles under Lincoln's eyes were as dark as his black chair. "We've all lost so much in battle," he said.

Lincoln gave Robert a sad smile. "This has been a nice break in a long day," he said. "Why don't you stay for dinner?"

Robert thought of the man wearing the perfect coat with shiny buttons. He imagined women in silk dresses. He had heard Mrs. Lincoln wore lace in her hair.

Robert was wearing brand new pants. But they could never hide his boots, all cracked and patched.

"No, sir," said Robert, "I am not dressed for such a fine occasion."

Lincoln's smile looked a little happier. He smoothed his coat, which was very rumpled.

He pulled his crooked tie back where it belonged.

"Do you know what they say?" said Lincoln. "It is not clothes that make the man."

Lincoln unfolded himself from his chair. He put his huge hand on Robert's shoulder.

"I'm hungry," he said. "Let's find out what we're having for supper."

Robert Henry Hendershot

History can be confusing.

We usually think what we read in history books is true. Yet history is really a combination of what happened and what people think happened. What people saw and what they wanted to see. What they did and what they remembered doing.

Years later it's hard to know what is fact and what is folktale.

Robert Henry Hendershot was a real boy. He was born in Michigan in 1850. He really ran away from home to join the army. He really was a drummer boy at Fredericksburg.

William Sumner Dodge wrote a book about Robert in 1867. This book bragged so much that I didn't always believe it.

But a newspaperman at the Battle of Fredericksburg also wrote about Robert's adventures. General Burnside wrote a letter to Abraham Lincoln about Robert's bravery. Lincoln's records say that he met with Robert. Lincoln wrote a letter about this "very brave" boy as well.

As the author of this book, I added to Robert's story. I did not always know Robert's private thoughts or conversations. So I dreamed up a few. I knew that Lincoln liked Robert enough to invite him to dinner. And that Robert was ashamed of his clothes. I could only imagine the other things they talked about.

Robert wasn't the only boy who dreamed of war. In the beginning of the Civil War, boys had to be eighteen years old to join the Union army. Yet more than ten thousand underage boys snuck into uniform. Many wrote the number 18 on a piece of paper and put it in their shoes. Then they could honestly say that they were "over eighteen."

Most of these young volunteers became drummer boys. Like Robert they used their drums to announce the day's events, from wake up to bedtime. They also ran errands and helped cook. They helped bandage wounded soldiers. They carried these wounded men off the battlefield on stretchers.

They even helped bury the dead. Too many soldiers died in the Civil War—approximately 620,000. More American soldiers died in this war than in all of our other wars combined.

The Battle of Fredericksburg was a very bloody battle. Robert's part—helping the bridge builders—was a great success. The rest of it was a terrible defeat for the Union.

The Union army had gotten to the Rappahannock River in November. But General Burnside wanted to build several bridges across the river. The pontoons didn't arrive for almost a month. This gave the Confederate army enough time to set up on the hills outside Fredericksburg.

The actual battle was one of the largest our country had ever had. Union generals had a hard time getting clear messages to each other. Huge mistakes were made. Union soldiers were told to climb a hill. The Confederate army was at the top waiting for them, protected by a wall.

These Union soldiers didn't have a chance. One general said that his troops "melted like snow coming down on warm ground." By the end of that day, over 12,600 Union soldiers were wounded or captured or dead. The Confederates lost about 5,300 men.

The Union lost that battle but won the Civil War in 1865. The North and the South stayed one country, the United States of America.

This war was the last one to use drummer boys in battle. The noise of so many cannons made drums hard to hear. New rifles were so much better that men no longer faced each other on huge fields. Armies no longer needed drummer boys to pound out commands.

Robert was one of the last drummer boy heroes.

Further Reading

If you liked reading about Robert, drummer boys, and the Civil War, you can also try:

Brill, Marlene Targ. *Diary of a Drummer Boy.* Brookfield, Connecticut: The Millbrook Press, 1998.

Fleischman, Paul. *Bull Run.* New York: HarperCollins Children's Books, 1993.

Murphy, Jim. *The Boys' War: Confederate and Union Soldiers Talk About the Civil War.* New York: Clarion Books, 1990.

Osborne, Mary Pope. *My America, My Brother's Keeper, Virginia's Diary.* New York: Scholastic, Inc., 2000.

Polacco, Patricia. *Pink and Say.* New York: Philomel Books, 1994.